DENNIS the MENACE

THE GREATEST MENACE EVER!

published under licence by

meadowside
CHILDREN'S BOOKS

HORROR HOTEL

There was a very long queue of people leaving Dennis's house.

Some of them were clutching broken toys. Some of them were limping. All of them were carrying newly signed cheques.

"It's the same every week," growled Dennis's dad, as he put his chequebook away. "I have to pay for all the damage Dennis causes."

"You won't have to pay next week," said Dennis's mum. "A nice break by the seaside will do us all the world of good."

Mum had seen a cheap holiday in the travel agent's. Everyone was going – including Dennis's best mate Curly.

"Make sure you pack your catapult and peashooter, Dennis told Curly. "A menace must be prepared at all times!"

Three hours later the car pulled up at the hotel, piled high with bags and suitcases. A porter came out and helped carry their luggage inside.

In the lobby the receptionist looked down at Dennis and Curly. Her lip curled and her nose twitched. It twitched even more when she saw Gnasher.

There was a very cross-looking woman nearby. She was wearing a flowery blouse, a long flowery skirt and an enormous hat with huge fake flowers all over it. In her arms was a tiny, fluffy white dog. Gnasher growled and bared his teeth. It was just the sort of dog he hated.

"That's the Duchess of Porpington and her sweet little dog, Cuddles," whispered the receptionist in her excitement.

"Looks like an explosion in a florists with a ball of fluff to me," muttered Dennis to Curly. Mum glared at him.

To their delight, Dennis and Curly were sharing a room.

"I want you two to unpack," said Mum as she walked out. Dennis shook his head.

"Forget the unpacking!" Dennis chuckled. "We need to check out this hotel!"

They raced out of the room. On the ground floor they burst out of the lift, but the floor had just been polished. Dennis, Curly and Gnasher skidded and crashed into the porter. He fell over backwards, sending suitcases flying in all directions.

Dennis and Curly sat up on top of a pile of luggage. They saw a familiar face staring at them in horror. It was their oldest enemy, Softy Walter, with his parents and his friend Bertie Blenkinsop!

Walter's perfumed poodle, Foo-Foo, was prancing around at Walter's feet.

"Softy alert!" shouted Curly.

"D... D... *Dennis!*" stammered Walter. "What are you doing here?"

"We're on holiday," grinned Dennis, gleefully.

"You can't possibly be on holiday here!" wailed Walter. "We're on holiday here!"

A menacing smile spread over Dennis's face.

"This is gonna be a great holiday!" he chuckled.

"Let's check out the kitchens!" said Curly. "I wanna know what we're gonna be eating!"

Dennis and Curly raced into the dining room and through the double swing doors into the kitchen. The chef was standing over a hot oven.

He was red in the face and very fat. When he saw Dennis and Curly his face got even redder.

"I won't let children in my kitchen!" he bellowed.

"GET OUT!

you 'orrible little pests!"

Dennis and Curly ducked out of sight behind a cupboard and the chef thought they had left. Dennis noticed an enormous tub of black pepper. His eyes began to twinkle menacingly.

When the chef turned his back, Dennis and Curly lifted the tub of pepper and tipped its contents into the steaming saucepan of soup. They gave it a quick stir, then tiptoed out of the kitchens.

As they dashed out of the dining room they bumped into Dennis's mum and dad.

"Ah, there you are," said Mum. "We've left Bea with the hotel babysitter. Have you boys had lunch already? We're just going in."

"We're gonna explore the hotel," said Curly. They watched as Mum and Dad sat down. Mum ordered a salad, but Dad ordered soup. A grin spread across Dennis' face.

Dad took a big spoonful of soup and gulped it down. His face went pink, then scarlet, then purple with white spots. His eyes watered. Steam came out of his ears. His mouth opened in a loud roar. All around the room, the other people who had ordered soup were doing the same thing.

"Water!" gasped Dad, as soon as he could speak. He glugged down three glasses of water. Then he saw Dennis and Curly sniggering.

"Go to your room!"

bellowed Dad. "And stay there!"

Back in their room, Dennis and Curly leaned out of the window. They could see Walter and Bertie down below. Dennis reached into his back pocket.

"How about a bit of target practice?" he suggested. "Bet you can't hit Walter's ice cream!"

Curly pulled out his peashooter. "You're on!" he grinned.

Curly's first shot went wide and hit an old lady who was bending over to pat Foo-Foo.

"Oooh!" she squealed, clutching her bottom.

Dennis's shot whizzed under Walter's nose and into Bertie's ear.

"YOWEE!" yelled Bertie, clutching his ear.

"Ooops!" said Dennis, with a chuckle. "Missed!"

Curly took another shot and hit the bottom of the ice cream cone. Ice cream started to drip all over Walter's designer sandals.

"Yes!" cheered Curly. Dennis's next shot landed straight on top of Walter's ice cream. As Walter took a big lick he got the hard pea in his mouth and nearly broke his delicate teeth. Dennis and Curly were laughing so hard they had to hang onto the windowsill. But suddenly they heard a sound behind them. It was Mum and Dad!

"Dennis, why do you have to be such a menace?" yelled Dad.

Just then there was a loud scream from Mum and Dad's room. The hotel babysitter came running out. She had baby food splattered all over her head!

"I'm not looking after that little monster any more!" she howled, as she ran past.

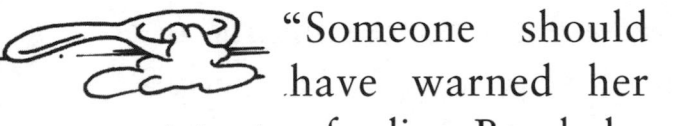

"Someone should have warned her not to try feeding Bea baby food!" chuckled Dennis.

"Well, if we don't have a babysitter, there's only one thing to do," said Mum.

"Dennis, you're looking after Bea for the rest of the day!"

Dennis stopped chuckling and Curly gave a loud groan. Gnasher bared his teeth.

"We're not babysitters," Dennis grumbled loudly.

"You are now!" said Dad. "We're going for a nice relaxing stroll. Don't get up to any more trouble while we're out!"

Dennis folded his arms as Mum and Dad went down the stairs.

"That's great," complained Curly. "Nothing to do but watch a baby!"

A grin slowly spread across Dennis's face. "You're not thinking like a true menace!" he said. "Bea's no ordinary baby... and we're not ordinary babysitters! I think she should have a bit of fun after all that yucky baby food!"

Dennis and Curly raced into the room and picked Bea up.

"We'll take you on a tour of the hotel, little sis'!" grinned Dennis, giving Bea a piggyback. They all headed downstairs.

In the lobby, Walter was talking to the Duchess of Porpington. Cuddles was sitting on her lap.

"It would be a pleasure to walk Cuddles for you, your ladyship," simpered Walter.

"I am a duchess, not a lady!" boomed the Duchess. **"You should call me 'your grace'!"**

"Oh yes, your grace," said Walter, bowing so low that his nose almost touched the floor.

"Sucking up already," Dennis grinned. "I think it's time we showed Cuddles what a real dog looks like!"

Gnasher shot over to the Duchess and Foo-Foo hid behind Walter. Cuddles yelped in terror at the sight of the Tripe Hound and tried to hide up the Duchess's blouse.

"EEK!" screamed the Duchess. "Get that revolting dog away from me!"

Gnasher chased Foo-Foo in circles around Walter. Foo-Foo's lead got tangled around Walter's legs and he crashed to the floor.

"Mumsy!" Walter wailed.

The Duchess of Porpington pulled Cuddles out of her blouse and marched up to Dennis, waggling her finger and looking crosser than ever.

"If you don't keep that fleabag of yours under control," she snarled, "I am going to complain to the manager and have you thrown out! I am a Very Important Person!"

"GNASHER DOESN'T HAVE FLEAS!"

Dennis yelled. The Duchess's nose was inches away from his. But Bea was still on Dennis's back, and she couldn't take her eyes off the Duchess's waggling finger. She leaned closer... closer... and...

"CRUNCH!" She champed down hard on the finger with her little white teeth!

"YOWEEE!" hollered the Duchess, clutching her finger.

"She's got a good set of gnashers!" grinned Dennis. "Let's go!"

"CRASH!" They ran out of the lobby. They bumped into the hotel porter again! Suitcases flew through the air. A birdcage skidded across the polished floor and burst open. Two budgies escaped and started flying in circles around the lobby.

"Help! Help!" squealed the receptionist. "I'm terrified of birds!" She hid under the check-in desk.

"Grrr!" fumed the porter.

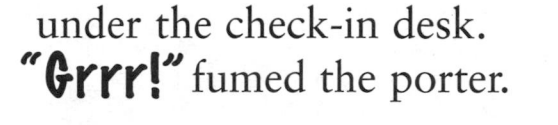

"Fun!" squealed Bea, waving her rattle around. But it hit the fire alarm on the wall next to her!

The alarm went off and the sprinklers came on, spraying water over everyone in the hotel!

"Evacuate! Evacuate!" screamed the hotel manager, running up and down the lobby. "Everyone out! Fire! Fire!"

The guests poured out of the hotel. The staff grabbed hoses in a panic and started spraying the hotel with jets of water. All the guests ended up being soaked to the skin.

It took half an hour for the staff to check the hotel and realise there wasn't a fire.

The receptionist came out of the lobby, holding Bea's rattle.

"There was no fire," she told the manager. "But I found this next to the broken fire alarm."

"Mine!" squealed Bea, snatching it from the receptionist. The hotel manager turned to look at her. His eyes popped. His face went dark red. **"You... you...!"** he stammered.

"Er, time to go!" said Dennis, scooting back into the hotel.

Back in their room, Bea bouncing up and down on Dennis's bed.

"Hungry!" she yelled, smacking Curly on the head with her rattle.

"Yeah, me too," agreed Dennis.

23

He picked up a menu that was lying next to the phone. "Aha! Room service!"

"I'm absolutely starving," said Curly, rubbing his head. Gnasher barked in agreement.

"Lobster surprise, ratatouille, sashimi, scallops, blah, blah... I don't even know what some of this stuff is!" said Dennis. "So we'd better order three of everything." Gnasher growled. "Sorry, Gnasher – four of everything!"

Down in the kitchen, the chef was very busy. He was making food for a special party and he was already late because of the fire alarm. When Dennis's order came in, his eyes bulged and his mouth dropped open in horror.

"Four of everything on the menu?"

he screamed. "Oh no!"

Soon the plates of food started to arrive in the room. Dennis, Curly, Bea and Gnasher tucked in as the plates and tureens stacked up around them.

"Try this one, it's delicious!" said Curly, dipping his spoon into the chocolate soufflé. Dennis tried to answer with his mouth full and sprayed lobster all over Gnasher.

"Good!" gurgled Bea, stuffing mashed potato into her mouth. Gnasher wolfed down an enormous steak. Two waiters staggered in, groaning under more plates of food.

When Dennis's mum and dad came back, they stopped outside Dennis's room and listened.

"It's very quiet in there," said Mum.

"I can't understand it," said Dad.

They turned the handle and the door swung open. Mum and Dad gasped in horror.

The room was piled up to the ceiling with plates, bowls and dishes of every size and shape! Scraps of food were scattered over the floor. And in the middle of it all lay Dennis, Bea, Curly and Gnasher. They were too full to move, with bulging tummies and huge smiles.

Dad went a very funny colour. He opened his mouth but couldn't make a sound.

BURP!

"DEN-NIS!" screeched Mum. "What have you done?"

Dennis gave a loud burp.

"Bea was hungry," he said. Bea gave a little burp too.

"What... who... where...?" stammered Dad. But before he could think of anything to say, there was a loud knock at the door and the hotel manager walked in. His face was purple and his fists were clenched.

"Your children have done more damage in one day than this hotel has ever known!" he fumed. "The guests have been soaked with water! The sprinklers have made the furniture warp!

"Our babysitter has had an attack of the vapours! Your daughter has bitten the Duchess of Porpington! Cuddles is having a nervous breakdown! My waiters are too exhausted to work! My head chef is hiding in the store cupboard! And my porter is too scared to carry any luggage!"

"But..." began Mum. The manager held up his hand to stop her.

"I have never thrown guests out of my hotel before," he said, through gritted teeth. "But there is a first time for everything! For the rest of the week I don't want to see those menaces in my hotel from breakfast to bedtime, otherwise they're **OUT!**"

He marched out and Dad glared at Dennis. "Do you hear that? From now on, you don't set a toenail in this hotel during the day!"

"We've had our fun in the hotel anyway," Dennis chuckled happily. "Tomorrow we'll find out what else there is to do around here. And with Bea we'll be able to get up to twice the menacing!"

JELLYFISH JOKER

It was the second day of Dennis's holiday. He and Curly walked out of the hotel with Mum, Dad and Bea. The hotel manager glared at them.

"Remember, I don't want to see either of you until bedtime!" he hissed. "And that goes for your menacing little sister too!"

"Suits me," grinned Dennis. "Mum and Dad want to spend the day on the beach, and we're gonna have some fun!"

Dad put his hand on Dennis's shoulder. He leaned down until their noses were touching. His eyes were red and popping.

"If you get up to any menacing today," he growled, "you'll be sorry."

"We're just gonna play on the beach," Dennis grinned. "No menacing in that, Dad."

Dad straightened up and Dennis winked at Curly.

"I'm sure we can think of something, though!" he whispered.

When they got to the beach, the sun was shining, the sky was blue and the sea was sparkling. Mum and Dad hired two deckchairs and leaned back in them.

"What a perfect day," sighed Mum.

"This holiday was such a great idea," Dad agreed.

"I hope Dennis and Curly are having fun," added Mum, looking up and trying to see them on the beach. They were nowhere in sight.

"Just as long as they don't get up to any menacing," yawned Dad.

"It's just a beach," Mum smiled. "How much menacing can they do on a beach?"

Five minutes later Dennis, Curly, Bea and Gnasher stood in a row, looking at Mum and Dad. They were already fast asleep in their deckchairs. Dad had a big hat over his face. Mum was snoring gently.

"They won't wake up for hours," Dennis chuckled, rubbing his hands together. "Plenty of time for a bit of seaside fun."

"Yeah," said Curly, crossing his arms. "But there's nothing to do."

"Don't be so sure," grinned Dennis, slapping Curly on the back. "Look who's over there." He pointed to where Walter the Softy, his dog Foo-Foo and Bertie Blenkinsop were busy building pretty sandcastles.

"I'm not playing with a bunch of softies," Curly grumbled.

"We don't have to play with 'em," said Dennis. "We'll just give 'em marks out of ten!"

They left Bea putting sand into Dad's sandwiches and walked over to Walter and Bertie.

"My sandcastle is perfect,"

Walter boasted.

He put a flag into the highest turret.

"My sandcastle is even bigger than yours," said Bertie. He stuck a big red bow on top of it.

Foo-Foo saw Gnasher and curled his lip.

"Our sandcastle is better than anything you nasty menaces could do!" he yapped.

"Oh yeah?" thought Gnasher. Dennis and Curly were busy judging the sandcastles.

"I'm knocking points off for the red bow," Dennis was saying.

"Go away!"

snapped Walter rudely.

"No one cares what you think!"

They weren't watching Gnasher. He started to dig! He dug a tunnel deep into the beach and underneath Walter and Bertie's sandcastles.

Foo-Foo pranced over and sat next to the sandcastles.

"Foo-Foo is the king of the castle!" Walter simpered.

Just then Gnasher gave a final dig and the sandcastles caved in! Walter, Bertie and Foo-Foo fell into Gnasher's tunnel!

"And Gnasher's the dirty rascal!" guffawed Dennis and Curly.

Suddenly they heard a loud braying. Not far away some donkeys were giving rides. The most spindly donkey looked very hot and tired. On his back was a big fat boy, waving his ice cream in the air and digging his heels into the donkey's boney sides.

"GEE **UP!**" he yelled. "Faster! Faster!"

The donkey gave a loud puff and rolled its eyes. Dennis frowned.

"Someone needs to teach that kid a lesson!" he said. "And I know just the teacher for the job!"

Dennis and Curly raced over to Mum and Dad.

"Dennis, it's your turn to look after your sister!" Dad ordered.

"No problem," Dennis grinned. "She's just what we need!"

They got back just as the fat boy slid off the exhausted donkey.

"That was rubbish," he complained. The donkey took a long drink of water and looked like it wanted revenge. Dennis tapped the boy on the shoulder.

"What?" snarled the boy.

"Is that your chocolate bar down there?" he asked, pointing at his feet.

"Chocolate?" the boy leaned down eagerly. The donkey took careful aim and planted a hoof in the middle of his bottom. As the boy fell forward, Dennis plonked Bea on his back and wound a skipping rope around his shoulders for reins.

"GIDDY **UP!**" squealed Bea, bouncing up and down and digging her sharp little heels in.

"Faster! Faster!"

"GER-**ROFF!**" roared the boy, trying to get up.

"If you don't give her a ride you'll have to give one to me and Curly – together!" bellowed Dennis. The boy scurried around the sand on his hands and knees, groaning each time Bea dug her heels in or pulled on the reins. The donkey was braying with laughter!

Finally Dennis lifted Bea off and the boy collapsed in the sand, puffing and panting.

Dennis chuckled . "Well done Bea – that'll teach that silly ass!"

They all went to get some ice creams, then walked back past the hot dog stand and Punch and Judy show.

The Punch and Judy man was just setting up.

Suddenly Gnasher spotted Punch's string of sausages hanging over the edge of the stand! With a delighted bark he leapt through the air. Dennis reached out to grab him but missed.

"**GNASHER NO!**" he yelled. "They're..."

Gnasher chomped on the sausages and gave a growl of fury.

"...plastic!" finished Dennis with a grin. Gnasher grabbed Punch and tore off down the beach, with the plastic sausages trailing after him.

"**Oi!**" bellowed the Punch and Judy man, chasing Gnasher.

"Leave him alone!"

roared Dennis, chasing the Punch and Judy man. They all pounded down the beach. Gnasher raced under deckchairs and leapt over people's heads. Mums and dads screamed and shouted as their picnics and children went flying. Hot on Gnasher's heels followed the furious Punch and Judy man, shaking his fists and bellowing. He stomped through the remains of

the picnics and trampled over the deckchairs Gnasher had knocked over. Dennis and Curly followed in a flurry of sand. Ice creams and cans of pop flew into the air and landed on the heads of screaming children.

Bea crawled after them as fast as her hands and knees could carry her. At the water's edge, Gnasher swung the sausages and Punch around his head, then opened his mouth. They whizzed into the air and out to sea.

"That'll teach him to tempt me with horrible fake sausages!" growled Gnasher.

"You rotten rascal!" shouted the Punch and Judy man, charging towards Gnasher. Dennis and Curly hurled themselves through the air and each grabbed one leg. The Punch and Judy man fell flat on his face into the sea and came up spluttering, with a huge piece of seaweed covering his eyes. He reached out his arms to grab them and they skipped out of his way, while Gnasher ran between his legs and tripped him over again.

"You... **YOU...!**" he choked, spitting sand and seawater. Dennis, Curly and Gnasher darted past him and back up the beach to where Dad was just pulling out his chequebook. A crowd of angry parents and screaming children was gathered around

him. Dennis, Curly and Gnasher skidded to a halt next to Bea.

"Er, we'd better come back later!" chuckled Dennis, seeing the steam coming out of Dad's ears.

"**POOL!**" gurgled Bea. She pointed over to the rock pools at the side of the beach. Dennis got a menacing twinkle in his eyes.

"Excellent plan, Bea," he grinned.
They raced over to the rock pools.
Dennis handed Bea a fishing net.

"See what you can catch," he told
her. "We're gonna explore!"

Curly and Dennis clambered over
the rocks to the furthest pools from
the beach. They filled their
 buckets with dozens of
rock pool creatures.
They found anemones,
 crabs, starfish and limpets.
When they
finally went back to Bea,
she had filled her net to
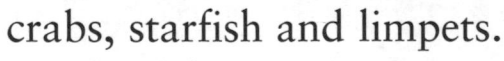 the brim with periwinkles,
baby crabs,
barnacles and
popping seaweed.

"Hot dogs!" said Dennis. "Let's go and get some ice cream! Then we'll think of something to do with our excellent catch!"

"Fizzy pop!" gurgled Bea.

"Hot dogs!" grinned Curly, and Gnasher licked his lips.

They scrambled back across the rocks towards the beach. But as Bea slid down on her nappy, the end of her net caught in a rock pool. The contents flew into the air and scattered all over the children who were playing nearby!

"Eeek!" squealed a little girl as a crab went down the back of her swimming costume.

Dennis and Curly tried to save the net, but they dropped their buckets! The air was filled with flying rock pool creatures!

"*Arghh!*" shouted a boy as a sea anemone tumbled down his swimming trunks.

The other children scattered, screaming, with crabs dangling from their noses and starfish stuck in their hair. Dad came storming over and grabbed Dennis and Curly.

"That's IT!" he roared, dragging them back to Mum. "You two are not moving for the rest of the day!"

Dennis looked sadly into his now empty bucket.

"All those menacing crabs – gone," he groaned.

"It's boring at the seaside," complained Curly. "No sharks, no manta rays, no octopuses. There aren't even any jellyfish!"

"Hmm," said Dennis, rubbing his chin thoughtfully. "You've given me an idea…"

Dennis and Curly waited until Mum and Dad were fast asleep again. Then they tiptoed up the beach and raced back to the hotel.

"We've gotta be careful," Dennis warned Curly and Gnasher. "If we're spotted, that horrible hotel manager will tell Dad and chuck us out for good!"

Curly and Gnasher followed Dennis around the back of the hotel and into the kitchen by the staff entrance. Inside they could hear the head chef yelling at his staff and clattering saucepans.

The table nearest to Dennis was covered with jelly, still in moulds. Dennis rubbed his hands together sniggering gleefully.

"These are gonna help us make the seaside a lot more exciting!" he whispered to Curly.

The chef was too busy screaming at his staff to notice what was going on in the corner of the kitchen. Slowly and quietly, two pairs of hands (and one pair of paws) reached up to the table. One by one they lifted the jelly moulds down until the table was bare.

The very smallest and youngest chef in the hotel kitchens was called Jamie. Jamie didn't like the head chef. He was always shouting at him and telling him off.

Jamie saw what Dennis and Curly were doing, but he didn't say a word. He just moved to one side to hide the table from the head chef's view, and he winked at Dennis and Curly. They grinned back at him and crept out of the kitchen, their arms filled with tottering jelly moulds.

Back on the beach, Dennis, Gnasher and Curly splashed into the sea and took the jelly out of the moulds. Green, red and yellow jellies bobbed on the waves.

"Man-of-war jellyfish!" yelled Curly, as a red blob of jelly hit Gnasher in the face. He doggy paddled after it and took a large bite.

"Box jellyfish! The deadliest in the world!" shouted Dennis, hurling a large blue jelly at Curly's head.

Suddenly they heard a piercing scream. One of the jellies was floating towards a wrinkly woman in a bathing cap. She had heard Curly's yell!

"Help! Help! Man-of-war jellyfish!" she squealed. "It's an invasion! Swim for your lives!"

Everyone in the sea started screaming as the brightly coloured jellies bobbed towards them. There was a rush for the shore. Surfers skimmed over the heads of bathers. Foam and spray were flung into the air by splashing arms and legs. There was a tangle of bodies on the shoreline as everyone scrambled up the beach.

Dennis and Curly guffawed. They waded out of the water with armfuls of jellies and walked towards the quivering crowd.

"It's just jelly!" Dennis tried to tell them, but they were screaming too loudly to hear him!

"They'll sting us all!" screamed Walter the Softy's mumsy.

"It's an attack!" the Punch and Judy man trembled.

"Call the police! Call the army and the navy!" cried the ice cream seller.

"RUN!" roared the hot dog seller.

There was a stampede and the crowd vanished up the beach in a whirl of sand and flip-flops. Dennis and Curly watched as they hurtled into the distance. Then they turned to each other and grinned.

"Are you thinking what I'm thinking?" asked Curly.

"Yep," said Dennis, licking his lips. "Those hot dogs are gonna go cold and the ice cream's gonna melt. We should help them out!"

"I think Gnasher's thinking the same thing too!" chortled Curly. Gnasher had taken a running jump onto the abandoned hot dog stand and was already halfway through the pile of sausages. Dennis and Curly raced over to the ice cream stall and helped themselves to double vanilla whips. Bea crawled up behind them and started to munch on the jellies. A huge flock of seagulls swooped down from the sky on the abandoned picnics and started to feast.

Behind them, Mum and Dad blinked and stretched.

"What a lovely sleep," said Mum.

"Very relaxing," Dad agreed. "The beach is very quiet... that's odd."

He stood up and shaded his eyes to look around. Then he spotted Dennis, Curly and Bea standing by the food stands.

Dad's fists clenched. His eyebrows waggled and his nostrils flared.

"DENNIS!" he hollered. Seagulls flew into the air in alarm. Crabs scuttled for cover. On the other side of the beach, Dennis and Curly glanced at each other.

"Time for a speedy exit!" Dennis said. They turned to run, but the crowd of people was coming back! They all looked very angry indeed. The Punch and Judy man had got a piece of man-of-war in his mouth by accident and found it tasted more like a raspberry than a jellyfish!

"There they are!" shouted Walter's mumsy.

"You're all banned!" the lifeguard fumed.

"GET THEM!" yelled the Punch and Judy man.

Dad was striding up the beach. The crowd was blocking the way off.

"We're trapped!" yelled Curly.

"What are we gonna do?" Dennis shouted.

"Birds!" chirped Bea.

The seagulls had finished their food and flown into the air. They had

never known such a feast and they were very grateful! With loud squawks they swooped down to where Dennis, Bea and Curly were standing. One of them took Bea's nappy in its beak and lifted her into the air! Four more picked Dennis and Curly up while Gnasher was whisked off the sand by one very fat gull. Dad and the crowd were too late. Dennis had escaped!

Dad turned to face the angry people. They took one step forward. He took one step back and felt the waves flow over his socks and into his sandals.

"Yes, he's my son," he groaned. "I'll just go and get my chequebook…"

GRUESOME GHOSTS

"Hurry up, Dennis!" called Mum. "We have to go!"

Dennis and Curly ran out of their hotel room, tucking their catapults into their back pockets.

"Banned from the hotel and banned from the beach," sighed Dad as they walked downstairs. "What shall we do today?"

Dennis pointed at a poster on the hotel noticeboard.

FUN FAIR!

Come and enjoy the best fun fair in the world!

HELTER SKELTER!
FERRIS WHEEL!
CANDY FLOSS!
CAROUSEL!
DODGEMS!
HOOPLAS!
AND MUCH MUCH MORE...

"A fun fair!" grinned Curly.

"Candy floss!" Bea gurgled.

"I'm not so sure this is a good idea," muttered Dad to himself.

"They can't get up to any menacing while they're having fun!" said Mum brightly.

"Wanna bet?" chuckled Dennis under his breath.

They walked out of the hotel. Dennis waved at the hotel manager, who was watching them from his office window. He glared back. As they walked past the beach they also got glares from the lifeguard, the Punch and Judy man and the ice cream seller. Dad gritted his teeth.

"Everyone knows you, don't they, Dennis?" said Mum.

Dennis and Curly just grinned.

When they reached the fun fair it was already really busy with holidaymakers. Loud music was playing and they could hear the screams of the people on the rides.

"Dad and I are going to have a cup of tea," said Mum. "You two have fun – and behave!"

"I promise we'll behave, Mum..." said Dennis.

Mum and Dad walked off with Bea and Dennis chuckled.

"...we'll behave like a couple of proper menaces!"

Dennis and Curly dashed into the fun fair and made a beeline for the hoopla. There were lots of different games to play.

"Roll up! Roll up!" shouted the woman in charge of the firing range. "Three shots for only a pound! Hit the target with the cork pistol!"

"I'll bet I hit every target!" grinned Curly, picking up a cork gun. "I'm the best shot in Beanotown!"

"Only when I'm not there!" chuckled Dennis, grabbing another cork gun.

TWANG!

Curly's first shot missed the target, hit the back of the stall and bounced back into the stallholder's head.

"Watch it!" she yelled, rubbing her head. Dennis guffawed.

"Best shot in Beanotown? Watch this!" He took aim, stuck his tongue out to help him concentrate and fired.

PYANG!

The cork shot through the back of the tent and lodged in the ear of the stallholder behind!

"Oi!" he roared at the woman. "Keep your customers under control!"

Curly's next shot skimmed across the top of the target and up the stallholder's left nostril. She yelped and tried to pull it out, as Dennis's next shot went up her right nostril.

"You two pests!" she growled, tugging at the corks.

"These cork guns are useless," complained Dennis. "They don't fire in a straight line! I'm gonna use my own weapon instead!"

Curly and Dennis pulled their catapults from their back pockets and loaded the corks into them. They fired at exactly the same time and both hit their targets!

"Yes!" cheered Curly. "What's our prize?"

"A visit to the police station if I catch you!" bellowed the stallholder, who still couldn't get the corks out. She charged towards them but they ran into the crowd and escaped!

The next stall had a row of moving plastic ducks and a water pistol.

"Hit five ducks with the water pistol and win a prize!" called the stallholder. "Come on, don't be shy!"

Dennis and Curly pounded up and grabbed the water pistols. They hit the ducks with one shot, but there were still two pistols full of water left!

"Can't waste it!" chuckled Dennis, turning on Curly – but he had the same idea! They fired on each other at the same time and were both knocked backwards. With water in his eyes, Dennis couldn't see where he was firing. Gnasher leapt out of the way as he and Curly tried to hit each other. Stallholders and holidaymakers hid under tables and behind stalls as the powerful jets of water hit them at full blast! When the pistols were empty Dennis wiped the water out of his eyes and looked around in surprise.

"Hey, where'd everyone go? And where's my prize?"

"I'll give you a prize!" snarled the sopping stallholder, leaping out and chasing the two menaces. They disappeared into the crowd and headed for the dodgems.

"Wheeeeee!" yelled Curly as he rammed into Dennis's bumper car. "Gotcha!"

Dennis whirled his car around as Gnasher held onto the steering wheel with his teeth. They charged straight at Curly, but at the last minute Curly dodged out of the way. Dennis was going so fast that the edge of the arena didn't stop his car! It flew through the air and landed next to the fortune-teller's stripy tent.

"You menace!" yelled the dodgem car owner. "You've ruined my dodgem car! Come back here!"

"Uh-oh!" said Dennis, looking around. There was a sign on the fortune-teller's tent that said "Out to lunch – back soon". Dennis gave a grin and slipped inside.

Two minutes later the dodgem owner burst into the tent. But all he found was a gypsy fortune-teller sitting behind a crystal ball. She had a shock of black hair and a lacy scarf covering her nose and mouth.

"Where's that rascal and his dog?" demanded the man.

"There are no rascals here, only your future," said the gypsy, stifling a giggle. The man sat down.

"What do you mean?"

"Look deep into the crystal ball!" said the gypsy. "I see a dark-haired stranger – he will make fun of you!"

"That pest!" fumed the man.

"He will trick you and make everyone laugh at you!" the gypsy warned in a trembling voice. "There is only one way to stop him!"

"What is it?" cried the man. "Tell me! Please! "

"You must leave the dodgems at once!" the gypsy ordered in a ringing voice. "Go and don't come back until midnight!"

"I will!" he cried, jumping to his feet, quickly.

"Oi! Cross my palm with silver!" croaked the gypsy. The man threw a handful of coins on the table and ran out of the tent.

"Ho ho!" guffawed Dennis, pulling off the lacy shawl. Gnasher jumped off his head. "You make a good wig, Gnasher!"

Dennis found Curly standing by the Ferris wheel.

"That oldie ride's too slow for me!" said Dennis. "Let's try the waltzers!"

After they had been on the waltzers three times and had eaten five hot dogs each, they saw a punchball game. Dennis gave it a hard thump and **THWACK!** It bopped Curly on the nose!

"Hey!" he cried. "You're not supposed to hit me!"

"You shouldn't stand in the way!"

chuckled Dennis. "How about the bouncy castle?"

They raced over to the bouncy castle, but the man in charge held out a large, grubby hand.

"Not so fast," he rumbled. "I don't like the look of you and we don't allow dogs on here. Clear off!"

"We don't like the look of you, either!" said Dennis. But the man just folded his arms. Dennis and Curly went around the corner.

"Time for a bit of plotting and planning," Dennis said. "I'll plot and you plan."

Five minutes later the bouncy castle man saw a piece of paper flutter to his feet. He bent down and picked it up. It said, "I know how you can become the owner of the whole fun fair. If you want to know more, come to the fortune-teller's tent right now."

The man's eyes nearly popped out of his head! It was his dream to own the fun fair. Then he could get rid of all the pesky children and just go on the rides himself! He took a quick glance around.

"This thing can do without me for five minutes," he muttered. He strode off to find the fortune-teller.

As soon as he was out of sight, Dennis, Gnasher and Curly raced around the corner and into the bouncy castle!

"Great! Gnasher's never been in one of these before!" shouted Dennis, as he bounced up and down in his heavy boots.

"He looks like he's enjoying it!" laughed Curly. Gnasher was bouncing so high he was hitting the roof of the castle!

Suddenly there was a hissing, whining noise. Gnasher's claws had made holes in the castle and it was losing air!

"Help! It's collapsing!" screamed the other children, jumping out just in time.

"Come on Gnasher," grinned Dennis. "Time to go!"

As they ran from the bouncy – er floppy – castle they bumped into Mum and Dad.

"We're just going on the Ferris wheel," said Mum.

"Dennis, you can look after Bea while we're on the ride"

She plonked Bea into Dennis's arms and walked off with Dad. Bea grinned toothily and gave Dennis a friendly whack with her rattle.

"Where next?" asked Curly, looking around. The dodgems were closed, the hooplas were in tatters and the bouncy castle was deflating.

"It looks like we've been on everything!" Dennis laughed. "Hang on a minute – look over there!"

In the corner of the fun fair was a ghost train. Dennis and Curly raced over to it. The sign read...

MUMSY'S MILD GHOST TRAIN
FOR THE TIMID AND SOFT.
(NO SHOCKS GUARANTEED!)

Walter and Bertie were already in the queue of softies.

"This sounds like the best ride in the whole fun fair,"

Walter said in a loud voice.

"My mumsy doesn't like me going on scary rides,"

agreed Bertie. Dennis and Curly grinned at each other.

"I think we should help this fun fair out," said Dennis. "Whoever heard of a ghost train that isn't scary? We need to liven it up a bit!"

Everyone climbed into the train and the ride began. First they went through some dangling cotton wool curtains. Then they heard a sugary sweet voice.

"Don't be afraid, little softies," it said. "We promise nothing bad will happen to you in here. You are about to see a sweet little skeleton – so don't jump!"

A skeleton with pink flowers painted on it swung out in front of the train.

"Oooh!" squeaked Walter. "It's a bit frightening!"

"Silly!" shouted Bea at the top of her voice.

"I've had enough of this," whispered Curly. "Let's show them what a real ghost train's like!"

They jumped out and ran ahead of the train. Dennis found the tape with the sugary sweet voice on it and turned it off. Then he picked up the microphone.

"This is the voice of doooom!" he said in a deep, echoing voice. All the softies clutched at each other in fright. **"Prepare to meet a fate worse than death!"**

"**Mumsy!**" screamed Walter. "Get the water bombs!" whispered Dennis, and Bea pulled them out. Curly took some long strips of wet seaweed out of his rucksack.

84

"I picked these up at the beach yesterday!" he chuckled. "Thought they might be useful!"

Dennis and Curly dangled the wet seaweed across Walter's face and along Bertie's arms.

"The ghost of the sea has you in her clutches!" boomed Dennis into the microphone.

"I want my teddy!" wailed Bertie.

Bea hurled the water bombs and they exploded all around the train, splashing everyone with icy water. Cries of horror came from the train! Gnasher howled like a werewolf and Dennis chuckled as he heard all the softies' teeth chattering.

The train was almost through the ride now, but Dennis dangled Bea upside down by the exit and she pulled the softies' hair and cackled like a witch.

The train left with the softies huddled down and screaming. Dennis, Bea and Curly roared with laughter as the ride ended.

"Let's wait for the next lot of softies!" grinned Dennis. "We've still got loads of spine-chilling water bombs left!"

Dennis's mum and dad had finished their ride on the Ferris wheel and were looking for Dennis and Bea. They visited the hoopla and saw the mess. There was water everywhere and one stallholder still had a cork stuck up her right nostril.

The other stallholder was trying to pull it out with pliers.

"He's been here," said Dad grimly.

"Just don't tell them we're his parents!" whispered Mum.

Dad quickly hid his chequebook. "I don't think this holiday was such a great idea!" he grumbled. "I'm more relaxed when I'm at home!"

Outside the ghost train, the angry fairground owner was putting on a fancy dress outfit.

He had heard about Dennis's menacing and was out for revenge.

Inside the ghost train, Dennis was getting bored. The train hadn't been through for ten minutes.

Suddenly, an icy cold wind swept through the dark chamber. There was an eerie creaking sound. Curly felt the little hairs on the back of his neck tickling.

"Wh... what was that?" he asked.

"Nothing," said Dennis. "Just someone opening a door."

Then a long sigh echoed through the chamber.

"Er, is there anybody there?" asked Dennis.

There was another cold breeze, then an icy hand clamped down on Dennis's shoulder. He turned slowly and found himself staring into the face of...

"A real vampire!" yelled Dennis.

"BRILLIANT!

"You're my dinner!" screeched the vampire, baring its long fangs.

"AWESOME!"squealed Bea.

"Eh?" said the vampire.

"MEGA!"roared Curly.

"Hang on a minute..." said the puzzled vampire.

"Catch it!" they all yelled together. Dennis made a grab for the vampire and it backed away in terror.

"Why aren't you lot scared" it trembled. "You menaces!"

"We're not scared of silly old vampires," yelled Dennis as Gnasher gave a menacing growl.

"In that case, I'm off!" said the fairground owner, as he vanished in a puff of smoke.

Dennis guffawed.

"We're the greatest menaces in the world!" he chortled. "Even the ghosts are scared of us!"

Written by RACHEL ELLIOT

Illustrated by BARRIE APPLEBY

published under licence by

meadowside
CHILDREN'S BOOKS
185 Fleet Street, London, EC4A 2HS